THE GREEN MAN

written and illustrated by Gail E. Haley

Charles Scribner's Sons · New York

Copyright ©1979 Gail E. Haley

First American edition published 1980

Library of Congress Cataloging in Publication Data
Haley, Gail E.
  The green man.
  SUMMARY: A rich, arrogant youth's enforced stay
in the forest changes his once selfish life into a
useful, generous, and satisfying one. Based on the
legend of "The Green Man."
  (1. Conduct of life—Fiction) I. Title.
PZ7.H1383Gr   (E)   79-20490
ISBN 0-684-16338-1

1 3 5 7 9 11 13 15 17 19 RD/C 20 18 16 14 12 10 8 6 4 2

  Printed in the United States of America

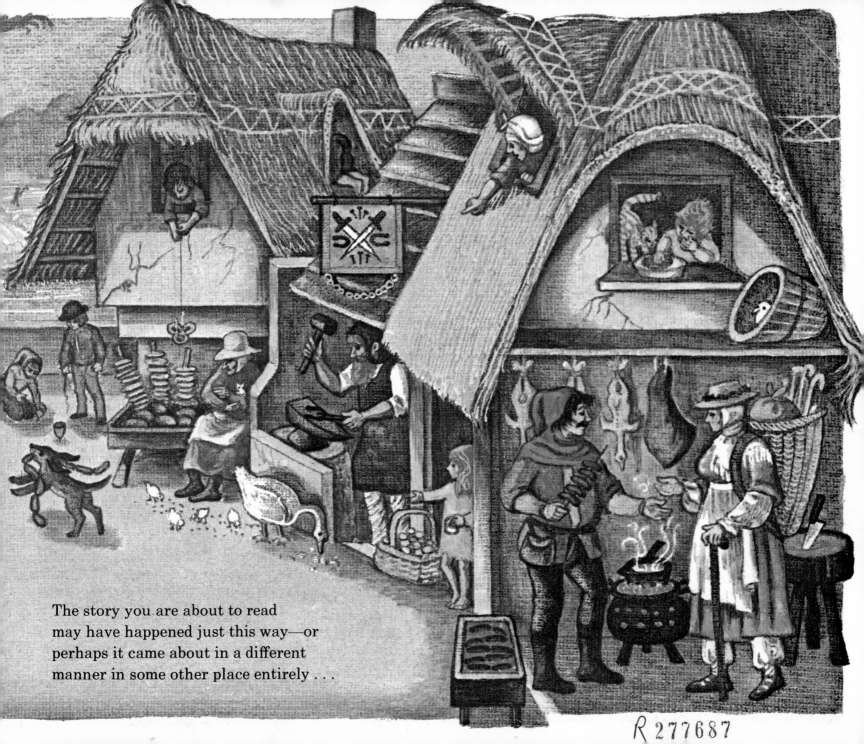

The story you are about to read
may have happened just this way—or
perhaps it came about in a different
manner in some other place entirely . . .

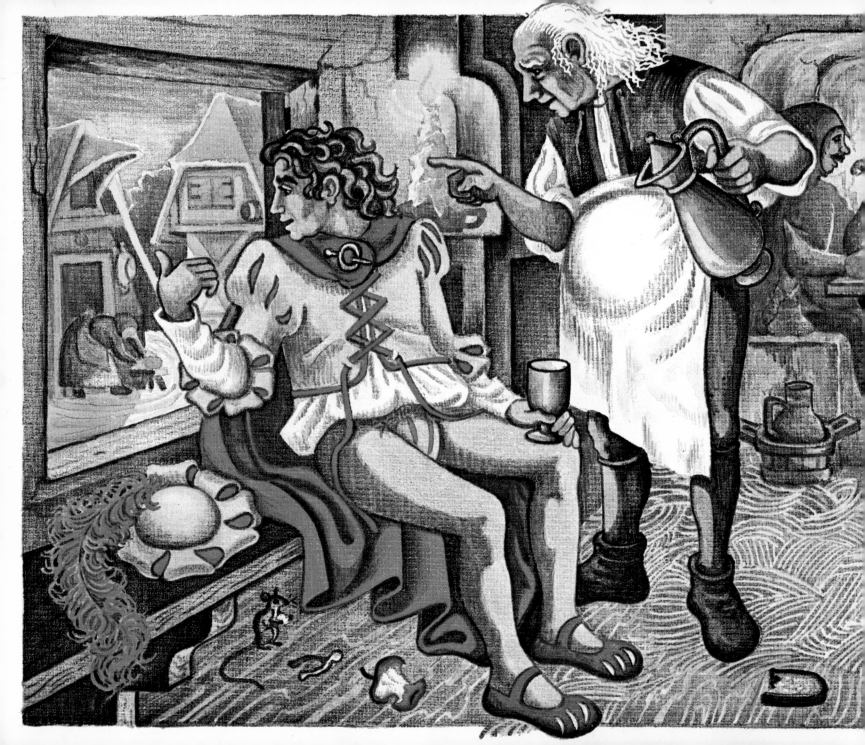

Claude was the only son of Squire Archibald. He was arrogant, vain, and selfish. He spent most of his time hunting, hawking, and riding about the countryside in his fine clothes.

One evening Claude rode into the village, and after ordering a lavish meal at *The Mermaid and Bush*, he sat watching the bustle of village life.

"Look at those ignorant peasants putting food out for the Green Man when they can barely feed their own children."

"They are grateful, Master Claude," replied the landlord. "For the Green Man keeps their animals healthy. He protects their children if they stray into the forest. Without him, the crops would not grow, nor the seasons turn in their course."

"Rubbish! Those are just silly tales. There is no Green Man!"

"Mind your tongue, sir," chided the landlord. "Terrible things can happen to those who make fun of old beliefs."

Some days afterward, Claude set out for a day's hunting. He never hunted on foot; he preferred to shoot from horseback. His men and dogs had gone ahead as beaters to drive the game toward him, but nothing was happening, and Claude grew tired of waiting. He rode deeper into the forest.

"Those beaters are incompetent. I haven't seen an animal all day!" he grumbled.

Soon Claude was hopelessly lost. It was hot, and his clothes felt heavy, when through the trees he saw a shady pond. Tethering his horse to a tree, he stripped off his clothes and dived into the cool water. He did not see a thin bony hand reaching out of the bushes.

Claude came out of the water refreshed and hungry, but on the bank he found nothing but a coil of rope.

Claude tied some leafy branches around his waist with the rope. Then he ate some of the strawberries that were growing on the bank. Feeling better, he chose a stout branch as a walking stick, and set off to find his way home. But as the day drew to a close, Claude realised that he would have to spend the night in the forest.

Peering about in the gloom, he saw before him the entrance to a large cave and felt his way inside. As he grew accustomed to the dark, Claude realised that he was not alone. There seemed to be something with glittering eyes and sharp horns near the mouth of the cave.

"Stay back! I'm armed!" Claude shouted. But the creature came no closer. Then something moved near the back of the cave. Claude clutched his stick for protection and drew his legs up onto a ledge. He lay there until, exhausted, he fell asleep.

When Claude woke it was morning and a little nanny goat was standing before him, tossing her head. He laughed with relief. It must have been she who had been at the back of the cave in the night.

Claude looked around. A young rooster was pecking busily near a nest full of eggs. A clay jug and a stone ax hung on the wall above Claude's head. Several rough baskets stood on the floor, and there was ash from a recent fire.

"This is someone's home," thought Claude. "Perhaps I should feed the animals." He gave the hens some grain which he found in a bowl, and picked some fresh grass for the goat as a special treat. Then he helped himself to goat's milk and eggs.

The goat nuzzled his hand, and he scratched her behind the ears. She frisked about and followed him when he set off to explore.

Not far away, Claude found a bees' nest in a tree, its honeycomb shining from inside the hollow trunk. Covering his body with mud to protect himself from stings, he climbed up to collect some honey.

Just then, a party of his father's men broke through the trees, blowing their horns and hallooing for him.

"They'll think I've gone mad, if they see me sitting in a tree covered with mud," thought Claude. "I can't let them see me without my clothes and my boots. I would be disgraced!"

So he let the party pass without revealing himself. Then he climbed down from the tree and crept back to the cave, followed all the time by the goat.

"I'll borrow something to cover myself from the owner of the cave when he returns and then I'll set off for home again," Claude said to his new friend, the goat. But time passed, and no one came. Claude lived on in the cave, growing leaner and stronger every day.

As the warm days went by, Claude forgot altogether about clothes. He nearly forgot that he was Claude, the Squire's son. He became Milker-of-the-Goat, Feeder-of-the-Hens, Friend-of-All-Wild-Animals. The forest creatures were not afraid of him. He fed them, talked to them, and spent hours watching them hunt and play.

As the berries, fruits, and nuts ripened, Claude became Gatherer-and-Preserver. When the grain was harvested in distant fields, he became Gleaner, venturing out at night to gather the leftovers for himself and his animals.

Claude was enjoying his new life. Even the sun and the moon seemed to smile upon him.

One morning, after a heavy rainstorm, Claude heard a frantic bellow coming from the direction of the river. He hurried there to see what was wrong, and found a cow who had been separated from her calf. They had taken shelter from the rain in a hilltop thicket, and as the water rose the river had surrounded them, turning the hillock into an island. The terrified calf would not follow its mother through the swirling current, and the cow was mooing loudly for help.

Claude waded across the water, picked up the calf, and carried it to its mother. Gratefully, the cow licked his hand, and then led her calf away through the forest toward the safety of the farmyard.

As the days grew colder, Claude added more ivy leaves to his costume. He tucked strips of moss and lichen between them to keep out the cold. He pounded birch bark to make it soft, and sewed pieces together to make a curtain for the mouth of the cave. After several attempts he even succeeded in making himself some birch-bark boots.

He built a fireplace near the entrance. He had found stones the right size and shape to make a mortar and a pestle, and each day he ground grain or nuts or acorns into flour. The smell of baking bread filled the air. A family of hedgehogs moved in.

The cave was now well stocked with food. Strings of mushrooms, parsnips, wild onions and herbs hung on drying poles. Claude made slings for the fruit and vegetables he had gathered. He formed barrels out of bark to hold apples and roots. Baskets of nuts, grain, and seeds were stored on a shelf above his mossy bed.

One day when Claude was out gathering acorns, he encountered a fierce wild boar threatening two small children from the village.

"Don't be such a selfish swine!" Claude spoke firmly to the boar. "There are enough acorns for everyone. Go away, and let the children have their share."

The boar snorted defiantly, but turned and trotted back into the forest.

"There, there, don't cry. The old boar is gone now." Claude comforted the children.

The girl looked up through her tears at the tall, sunburned man. He seemed as ancient, green, and moss-covered as the oak tree that towered above them.

"Are you the Green Man?" she asked in a whisper.

Claude looked down in surprise. Warm sunshine caressed his hair. A gentle breeze rippled his leafy costume. His feet felt as if they were rooted in the earth.

"Yes," Claude answered her at last, "I am the Green Man."

He helped the children to gather up their acorns and filled their basket to the brim. Then he led them safely to the edge of the forest.

When winter came, at night Claude visited the nearby sleeping villages. He helped himself to some of the food put out for him, but always left some for hungry, prowling animals. At times he felt lonely as he walked through the deserted streets, looking into the windows of the cosy houses. He was homesick for his own village and his family. But he returned each night to his cave and his animals. He was needed now in the forest.

Winter passed and spring was on its way. The smell of budding leaves, warm earth, and growing things filled the air. The days went by, and when he knew that the strawberries would be ripening by the pond, Claude went to pick them.

A man was splashing in the water. A fine suit of clothing lay on the bank and a handsome horse was tethered nearby.

Claude quietly took off his leaves and put on the clothes. He found shears and a glass in the horse's saddlebag, so he cut his long hair and trimmed his beard. Then he rode through the forest until he found his own home.

His mother and father were amazed and delighted to see him. Everyone thought that he had been killed long ago by robbers or eaten by wild animals.

"It was the Green Man who saved my life" was all that Claude would say.

His year away had changed the arrogant young man. Now he was hospitable to travelers. He cared for his animals. And each night Claude set out food and drink for the Green Man.

WHO IS THE GREEN MAN?

Legend tells us that there will be a Lord of the Forest "for as long as the Greenwood stands." It is certainly easy to believe that the Green Man is there—hidden among the leaves, watching to make sure that all is well. But who is the Green Man? Countless pub signs in Great Britain carry the portrait of the Green Man, dressed in his suit of leaves, striding from the forest with his staff sprouting in his hand. He peers down from the vaulted roofs and pillars of great cathedrals throughout Europe. And his mysterious haunting face, with its beard of leaves, is found in carvings from Lebanon to Rumania.

In heraldic emblems, the Green Man often appears hand in hand with mermaids. Early tapestries portray him riding a unicorn, or leading a fierce dragon as if it were a puppy. Ballads tell us that he was fierce in battle but kind to wounded knights, lost children, and damsels in distress. He was able to foretell the future, to heal wounds and sickness.

The Green Man had many names: Woodwose, Jack-in-the-Green, Wild or Savage Man, Woodhouse, and many others. Robin Hood and Puck were surely Green Men. Merlin was the son of a Wild Man and many of King Arthur's knights went into the forest to live as Green Men for a time. A twelfth century manuscript tells the story of Amleth, crown prince of the Danes, who went into the forest for a year with his friends, dressing in leaves and subsisting on roots, acorns, and wild fruit. Charles VI of France often went about dressed as a Wild Man and led his friends in wild romps through the streets of Paris. When Elizabeth I visited Kenilworth, "on the X (10th) of Julee, (1575) met her in the forest as she came hunting, one clade like a savage man all in ivie."

Perhaps the Green Man was originally Amaethon, the Celtic god of vegetation, the same god known to other cultures by such names as Dionysus, Osiris, and Gilgamesh. His origins are as mysterious as they are universal. We may never know who the real Green Man was . . . or who he will be next.